NIGHT WOLF

JONNY ZUCKER

ILLUSTRATED BY SEB CAMAGAJEVAC

Titles in Ignite II

Alien Harvest	Melanie Joyce
Blackbeard's Treasure	Roger Hurn
Chocolate Wars	Andy Seed
The Hamster Who Fell to Earth	Danny Pearson
Jimmy, Donkey of the Somme	Clare Lawrence
Night Wolf	Jonny Zucker
The Princess and the Knight	Helen Orme
Silent Screen	Mike Gould
Snow Beast	Craig Allen
Zombie Goldfish	Danny Pearson

Badger Publishing Limited
Oldmedow Road,
Hardwick Industrial Estate,
King's Lynn PE30 4JJ
Telephone: 01438 791037

www.badgerlearning.co.uk

2 4 6 8 10 9 7 5 3 1

Night Wolf ISBN 978-1-78147-455-6

Text © Jonny Zucker 2013
Complete work © Badger Publishing Limited 2013

All rights reserved. No part of this publication may be reproduced, stored in any form or by any means mechanical, electronic, recording or otherwise without the prior permission of the publisher.

The right of Jonny Zucker to be identified as author of this Work has been asserted by him in accordance with the Copyright, Designs and Patents Act 1988.

Publisher: Susan Ross
Senior Editor: Danny Pearson
Publishing Assistant: Jennifer Brough
Design: Fiona Grant
Illustration: Seb Camagajevac
Copyeditor: Ursula Faulkner

NIGHT WOLF

Contents

Vocabulary:

girlfriend	grabbed
muttered	sparkling
strolled	tense

Main characters:

Jenny

Felix

The werewolf

4

CHAPTER 1

A new face

Felix and Jenny were upset when their dad brought home his new girlfriend.

"This is Suzie," he said.

Suzie had bushy eyebrows, thick brown-grey hair and a low, growly voice.

"Nice to meet you both," smiled Suzie, showing her sparkling teeth.

"Hi," said Felix and Jenny together.

Dad put his arm round Suzie's shoulders. "Suzie is staying for supper tonight," he said.

Supper was awful. Suzie had a horrible deep laugh. She laughed at all of Dad's rubbish jokes. Felix and Jenny did not laugh.

After supper Suzie said she was going home. "Hopefully, I'll be spending more time with you," she said to Felix and Jenny.

"Hopefully, **not**" muttered Felix under his breath.

"She's great, isn't she?" beamed their dad after Suzie had gone and they'd done the washing up.

"She's ok, I suppose," said Jenny.

But Jenny was lying. She and Felix sat in her room that night and talked about Suzie.

"I don't like her bushy eyebrows," said Felix.

"Her laugh is horrible," said Jenny. "It gives me the creeps."

In the next few weeks, Suzie came to the house a lot.

Then, one night Dad told Felix and Jenny he had something important to say. "I've asked Suzie to move in with us," he grinned.

"Does she have to?" groaned Jenny.

"It will be great," said Dad. "You'll have a real chance to get to know her."

Two nights later Felix and Jenny heard a car pull up outside the house. It was Suzie. She opened the boot of her car. She grabbed several bags and hurried to the front door.

"I've got a bad feeling about this," said Jenny.

CHAPTER 1

A shocking arm

"Isn't this fun?" said Suzie after supper that night in her deep, growly voice. "Shall we play some board games?"

"Good idea!" nodded Dad.

"I've got homework," said Jenny, standing up from the table.

"Me too," said Felix, joining her.

"You never do your homework without being asked a hundred times!" cried Dad.

"We've got tests," replied Jenny.

That night before bed, Dad came and talked to Felix and Jenny. "Do me a favour?" he said. "I know it's hard but will you give Suzie a chance? She's a really good person."

"Fine," said Felix.

Jenny said nothing.

Over the next few days Felix and Jenny tried to steer clear of Suzie. But they could hear her deep, growly voice wherever they were.

At the weekend, Jenny was in the kitchen reading a book. Suzie was doing the washing up. She was wearing a long-sleeved t-shirt.

Jenny finished a page and looked up. For a second, Suzie's t-shirt arm lifted up a bit. Jenny saw Suzie's arm. It was covered in wisps of grey-brown fur.

Suzie quickly pulled her sleeve down.

Jenny pretended she hadn't seen anything. She waited a few minutes and then strolled out of the room. She found Felix in his bedroom.

"There's something really scary about Suzie!" she hissed.

"I know," nodded Felix, "her voice creeps me out."

"It's not her voice," said Jenny, "it's her arm."

She told Felix what she had seen.

"You're making it up!" said Felix.

"I'm not!" said Jenny.

On Saturday night, Jenny saw Suzie slipping out of the house very late.
I wonder where she's going? thought Jenny.

Just after midnight Jenny was woken by a distant howling sound.

"Felix!" cried Jenny running into his room. "Did you hear that sound?"

"What sound?" he asked, rubbing his eyes.

The sound had stopped.

"I think it's something to do with Suzie," said Jenny.

"Don't be crazy," said Felix sleepily, "it was just a bad dream. Go back to sleep."

But Jenny did not go back to sleep. Something was up with Suzie. And she was going to find out what it was.

CHAPTER 1

Howling at midnight

The next day at school, a kid called Nick came up to Felix and Jenny.
"Did you hear what happened last night?" he asked.

"No," replied Felix.

"Mac Thompson saw a werewolf on the common!"

"Don't be stupid!" said Felix.

"It's true," insisted Nick.

"It was a full moon last night," said Jenny.

"Werewolves don't exist!" cried Felix.

Nick walked off. Jenny grabbed Felix's shirt. "It was Suzie!" she hissed.

"What was?" asked Felix.

"The werewolf!" snapped Jenny. "Suzie is the werewolf!"

"I don't like her either," said Felix, "but that's mad."

A few weeks later when Felix was looking out of his bedroom window at night, he saw Suzie in the garden.

She was eating something. Her teeth gleamed in the moonlight. They were sharp and long.

The next morning he told Jenny. "You were right!" he said. "I think Suzie *is* a werewolf!"

"We have to go and talk to Dad!" said Jenny.

They found him in the living room reading a newspaper.

"Dad," said Jenny, "have you ever noticed anything... weird... about Suzie?"

"No," replied Dad, putting his paper down.

"You know," said Felix, "things about her... body."

Dad stood up crossly. "That's enough you two!" he snapped. "You've got Suzie all wrong!"

It was a full moon the next night. Jenny and Felix stayed up late.

At 11:45 p.m., they saw Suzie sneak out of the house.

"Let's follow her," said Jenny.

They grabbed their coats and ran out of the house. There was no sign of Suzie.

They ran to the common. They got there five minutes before midnight.

Everything was quiet.

But as midnight arrived there was a terrible howling from nearby.

Before they could say anything, they heard a terrifying roar and a werewolf came leaping through the air, right at them.

CHAPTER 4

Attack in the dark

"NOOOO!" yelled Jenny, but the werewolf had knocked Felix over.

"AAARRRGGHH!" shouted Felix, trying to push the werewolf off him.

But it was too strong. It opened its jaws and licked its lips.

WHACK! Jenny smashed the werewolf on the back of the head with a big branch she'd found on the ground.

The werewolf yelped in pain and crashed backwards off Felix.

"RUN!" screamed Felix.

Jenny and Felix had never run so fast.
They made it home in five minutes.

Sprinting inside, they slammed the door
shut and stood there panting and
shaking. Dad wasn't in.

"I bet he's gone out to find her," said
Jenny.

"What if she attacks him?" asked Felix.

The next morning Suzie wasn't around.

Felix, Jenny and Dad were in the
kitchen.

"Look, Dad," said Jenny. "There's something we have to tell you about Suzie."

"I don't want to hear anything mean!" snapped Dad.

"Dad!" pleaded Felix. "Suzie is a WEREWOLF! She attacked us on the common last night."

"We only just got away!" cried Jenny.

"You don't understand!" shouted Dad. "Suzie is NOT a werewolf!"

He stormed out of the room.

Things in the house were very tense for
the next few weeks.

When the next full moon appeared,
Felix and Jenny kept their eyes on
Suzie. That night she went out early.

When it was close to midnight they
heard their dad opening the front door.

They raced downstairs.

"Please don't go to her, Dad!" said Jenny.

"She might attack you!" cried Felix,
grabbing Dad's arm.

"STAY OUT OF THIS!" shouted Dad. He threw Felix off and ran out of the door.

"QUICK!" shouted Felix, "we've got to save him!"

But Dad had a head start and they couldn't see him. They raced to the common but suddenly halted in fear.

It was midnight. A spine-tingling howling sound was coming from nearby.

A few seconds later a werewolf came leaping out at them. But before it reached them, someone jumped into its path. It was... Suzie.

CHAPTER 5

The true werewolf

"YOU NEED TO STOP!" she shouted at the werewolf.

It bounded towards her. But she managed to grapple it to the ground.

She held it firmly in her arms. It howled for a minute and then just lay there, making snuffly noises.

"I don't get it," said Felix kneeling down, "we thought you were the werewolf."

"I am one," replied Suzie, "but I've been trained not to attack anyone."

"So who is this werewolf?" asked Felix.

"It's... it's your dad," said Suzie quietly.

The werewolf made a whimpering noise and looked at the children.

Jenny put out a hand and stroked the werewolf on the top of its head.
It looked at her sadly.

"That's how we met," said Suzie. "Your dad needed someone to train him not to attack."

"And you are the right person?" asked Jenny.

Suzie nodded.

"I'm sorry we've been horrible to you," said Felix.

"We were scared of you," said Jenny. "We thought you wanted to hurt Dad."

Suddenly, the werewolf on the ground began to change – first its face, then its body. It slowly became Dad again.

"Thank you," he said weakly, standing up. The others stood too.

"We're going to help Suzie train you," said Jenny.

Felix nodded. Dad smiled at them both.

The four of them turned and began the walk home. And this time when Suzie laughed her growly laugh, it wasn't horrible or scary.

It was warm and comforting.

Werewolves

Werewolves have been mentioned in folk tales and stories for thousands of years. A werewolf is usually a creature that can change from a human being into a wolf-like animal and then back to a human again.

In Ancient Greece it was said that every man in the Neuri tribe turned into a werewolf once a year. They stayed as werewolves for several days and then became men again.

The Ancient Greeks also thought they had a way of stopping men from becoming werewolves. They believed that if the men did lots and lots of exercise this would stop it happening. So they made suspected 'werewolves,' do hours and hours of running, jumping and lifting.

Over the years more and more tales were told, and in 13th century France, many people believed that a nobleman called Bizuneh changed into a werewolf once a week.

Some people claim that there are certain ways you can spot if a human being is a werewolf. They point to people whose eyebrows meet at the top of the nose, have curved fingernails, possess low-set ears or walk with a swinging stride.

In some stories it claims that humans are not born werewolves, rather they can become them. One idea is that if a human drinks rainwater out of a footprint left by a werewolf, then that human will become a werewolf too.

There have been many films about people who turn into werewolves. The most famous film being *An American Werewolf in London.*

Questions

Why were Felix and Jenny upset in the first chapter?

Who was Suzie?

What made Jenny think that Suzie was a werewolf?

What woke Jenny up just after midnight in Chapter 2?

Where did the werewolf jump out at Jenny and Felix?

Who in this story are werewolves?

When do werewolves traditionally come out?